Where, Oh Where, Is Santa Claus?

Where, Oh Where,

Harcourt, Inc.

Orlando   Austin   New York

San Diego   Toronto   London

Is Santa Claus?

Written by
Lisa Wheeler

Illustrated by
Ivan Bates

www.HarcourtBooks.com

Library of Congress Cataloging-in-Publication Data
Wheeler, Lisa, 1963–
Where, oh where, is Santa Claus?/Lisa Wheeler; illustrated by Ivan Bates.
p. cm.
Summary: Santa Claus is missing, and a host of arctic animals searches for him in the snow.
[1. Missing persons—Fiction. 2. Animals—Fiction. 3. Santa Claus—Fiction.
4. Polar regions—Fiction. 5. Stories in rhyme.] I. Bates, Ivan, ill. II. Title.
PZ8.3.W5663Whe 2007
[E]—dc22   2006007003
ISBN 978-0-15-216408-9

First edition
A C E G H F D B
Printed in Singapore

In memory of
Grandpa Oren and Grandma Margaret Wheeler,
who made every day like Christmas
—L. W.

For Lucas and Clara
—I. B.

Stamping-tramping
reindeer feet
clomp and stomp through
polar sleet.

Step-by-step in
Christmas snow,
search for Santa.
Where'd he go?

Clip-clop, clip-clop, two-by-two.
Santa! Santa! Where are you?

Fuzzy-furry
polar ears
hear the hooves of
Santa's deer.

Whiskers twitching
in the snow.
Hurry, bunnies—
off you go!

Hip-hop, hip-hop, polar paws.
Where, oh where, is Santa Claus?

Harking-barking
seal-pup twins
coast along on
polar fins.

Flippers flopping.
Bellies glide.
Follow bunnies.
Slip and slide.

Flip-flop, flip-flop, polar two.
Santa! Santa! Where are you?

Swishing-swooshing
polar tail.
Pit-pat paws go
down the trail.

Trekking-tracking
foxy nose.
Sniffs for Santa—
off she goes!

Pit-pat, pit-pat, polar paws.
Where, oh where, is Santa Claus?

Bumbling-tumbling
polar cub
toddles from
his arctic tub.

Icy droplets
splash and spray.
Shake, shake, shake—
he's on his way!

Thump-bump, thump-bump, polar paws.
Where, oh where, is Santa Claus?

Ziggy-zaggy
tricky track.
Crisscross, crisscross,
doubles back.

Giant paws
in snowy drifts . . .
Who has left
these polar prints?

Flicking-kicking
funny feet.
Upside down
in polar sleet.

Stumble-fumble
in the snow.
Snowshoes wagging
to and fro.

Hurry-scurry, polar paws.
Rescue dear old Santa Claus!

Heave-Ho!

"Ho-Ho-Ho!"
says Santa Claus.
"Thank you, thank you,
polar paws!"

"Hurry, reindeer—
to the sleigh!"

Clip-clop, clip-clop . . .

The illustrations in this book were done in wax crayons
and watercolor on Fabriano Artistico paper.
The display type was set in Melanie.
The text type was set in Pumpkin and Catseye Bold.
Color separations by Bright Arts Ltd., Hong Kong
Printed and bound by Tien Wah Press, Singapore
Production supervision by Christine Witnik
Designed by Lydia D'moch